THE PIZZA PLACE GHOST

Written by Class 1-208
Illustrated by Duendes del Sur

visit us at www.abdopublishing.com

Reinforced library bound edition published in 2013 by Spotlight, a division of the ABDO Group, PO Box 398166, Minneapolis, MN 55439. Spotlight produces high-quality reinforced library bound editions for schools and libraries. Published by agreement with Warner Bros.-A Time Warner Company.

Printed in the United States of America, North Mankato, Minnesota.
102012
012013
 This book contains at least 10% recycled materials.

Cover designed by Madalina Stefan and Mary Hall
Interiors designed by Mary Hall

Library of Congress Cataloging-in-Publication Data
This book was previously cataloged with the following information:

Class 1-208.
Scooby-Doo! : the pizza place ghost / written by Class 1-208 ; illustrated by Duendes del Sur.
p. cm. -- (Scooby-Doo! Picture Clue Books)
Scooby-Doo and the gang find out if the pizza place is really haunted.
[1. Dogs--Juvenile fiction. 2. Restaurants--Juvenile fiction. 3. Ghost Stories. 4. Rebuses. 5. Haunted places--Fiction. 6. Mystery and detective stories.]
PZ7 .S4135 2000
[E]
2001269965
ISBN 978-1-61479-038-9 (reinforced library bound edition)

One day, was reading the

 .

"Listen to this," she said to ,

 , and .

"All the is missing from

Frank's Place."

" ? ?" said. "Like,

I want to eat! Let's go to Frank's

 Place!"

At the 🍪 place, 🐕 and his

friends sat down at a 🪑 .

Frank told them the story.

"At the end of the day, a 🚚

comes and brings me 🧀 ,"

Frank said.

"But when I come in the next

day, the 🧀 is always gone!

And I cannot make 🍪 without

🧀 !"

"I do not know what happens to the ," Frank said.

"Every night I put the away. Then I close all the . I put a big on the . No one can get in."

"No one but a !" said.

"Ruh-roh!" said . He hid under a .

"We need to look for clues,"

 said.

"It is the only way to find the

missing ," said.

 shook his head.

"Will you do it for a ?"

asked.

 jumped up.

"Let's split up," said.

 went into the kitchen.

"Like, I want something to eat,"

he said.

 took out some .

He took out a bag of .

He took out some .

He made a big mess.

"  !" said.

 followed the .

He bumped into .

"Look!" said . "A trail of

."

 and followed the

and the trail of  .

and bumped into .

"Look!" said . "A trail of

 ."

 , , and followed the

, the trail of 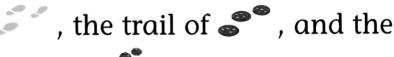 , and the

trail of .

The clues led them to the

kitchen.

"What are you doing, ?!"

said ,  , and .

 turned red. "I wanted

something to eat," he said.

"Where is ?" asked.

 did not know.

 was missing, too.

The gang went to look for .

The gang found .

He was using his to follow

a trail of !

The trail of led to a

in the wall.

 looked inside the .

looked back at .

Had found the ?

put his paw into the .

And what did he find?

 ! The had taken the

 !

Frank was happy. Now he could make .

And he made the biggest for and his friends!

Did you spot all the picture clues
in this Scooby-Doo mystery?

Reading is fun with Scooby-Doo!